I Don't

I Don't
Copyright 2022 by Colleen Hlavac

ISBN: 979-8-9853697-2-4

See more at:
www.colleenhlavac.com

I Don't

COLLEEN HOFSTADTER HLAVAC

See more at:
www.colleenhlavac.com

Instagram: @colleenhofstadterhlavac

Facebook: @thestalkerinthedesert

Email Address: colleenhlavac@gmail.com

For Andrea and Christian Hofstadter

1

BAR HARBOR, MAINE

Morning light poured into the coffee shop window. Brisk air whirled in behind Ivy as she entered and clicked the door shut. She bounded into their booth.

"Hey, Trevor! Hope you haven't been waiting long?"

"No, just got here…Glad I was able to snag our usual gossip booth."

The friends had been inseparable since preschool and this coffee shop had served as the backdrop for countless talks. Ivy affectionately referred to it as the shop of white cups and black coffee.

The scent of roasted coffee beans, sweet, warm caramel and chocolate confections saturated the air. Friendly banter and clinking cutlery echoed throughout the room. The coffee shop was packed with business people in crisp suits and a few straggling high school students. Ivy traced the top of her mug with her fingertip in endless circles.

"It's happening in five months, six days and seven hours, but who's counting?" Ivy giggled as she took another long, satisfying swig of her coffee.

"Can you believe it, Trev? I'm going to officially be Mrs. Ivy Westin before we know it. I'm so in love!"

"I know you are and I'm so happy for you… Brett's a lucky guy."

"I'm the lucky one. He's the greatest thing that has ever happened to me." She shook her head. "Still can't figure out how I landed such a good lookin' man."

"I hate when you put yourself down. You're the best. Brett won the lottery...Trust me on that."

"Trev, we both know that if anyone looks up 'average looking' in the dictionary, they see my face."

He opened his mouth but didn't get the chance to say anything.

Ivy raised her eyebrows. "My mundane looks are irrelevant, at this point. I'm happier than I've ever been in my life...and thank God every day that I'm engaged to the man of my dreams." She held her hands to her chest and almost swooned.

"Your happiness is most important to me... Which reminds me, did your work give you two weeks off for your wedding and honeymoon yet?"

Ivy grinned. "Yes! That's more good news I've been meaning to tell you. I just found out that the time off was approved yesterday... Everything is starting to come together. Brett graduates three weeks before our wedding."

They finished their drinks and exited into the bright, unforgiving sunlight of their hometown, Bar Harbor Maine.

Ivy had a five minute walk back to her work and her shift started in two minutes. Timeliness had never been one of her strong suits. She worked at the front desk of a beautiful, oceanfront, victorian style hotel. As a self-proclaimed extrovert, Ivy loved working in customer service, had cultivated several friendships and enjoyed meeting the hotel guests.

Ever since she was a teenager, her dream had been to become a doctor. Her plans changed when she met Brett in college.

They had attended the University of Maine in Orono together. He was two years ahead of her. After they became engaged, Brett urged her to return to Bar Harbor and start working in order to save money for their marriage. It took some convincing, but Ivy finally agreed to give up her dream of attending medical school. Her future marriage was her top priority, giving up her career aspirations made the most sense.

4

2

Maya's warm breath blew into Brett's ear causing him to stir from his unscheduled afternoon nap.

"Sweetie pie, you fell asleep. We have to get to class."

"How about we just blow off all our responsibilities and hang out in bed for the rest of the day?"

"Mr. Westin, you are such a naughty boy."

Brett grinned sheepishly and planted a tender kiss on her neck. "I know." The sound of an incoming text interrupted their amorous moment.

"Aw, ignore it, baby!" Maya pleaded. "It's probably that gross fiancée of yours anyway...I have one question. Why would you want chopped liver when you can have me...top sirloin steak?"

Brett chuckled as he glanced at his cell phone. It was a text from his future wife, Ivy.

Work is going smoothly. I haven't heard much from you today. Just want you to know how much I miss you.

Maya snatched the phone out of his hands and read the text.

"Ok, Brett, we need to talk. You've made it clear to me that you've felt lukewarm about Ivy from day one. The only reason you proposed to her is because your parents adored her and they were pressuring you...You don't love her. Are you seriously going to go forward with this joke of a wedding?"

"Actually, I have a surprise for you. I'm scheduled to go visit Ivy in two weeks. I'll break up with her then... After that, you and I can be together for life. I'm so excited!...Hope you are too?"

"Well, that is something to celebrate." Maya nuzzled his neck.

She got up and sauntered to the other side of the room to retrieve champagne.

Brett stared at her incredible body. Her long, shapely legs, sculpted abs and curves in all the right places would make any man melt into a puddle. Her wavy, raven-black hair hit mid-back. Olive skin and large, almond shaped, grey eyes mesmerized him. He could never seem to get quite enough of her.

3

Ivy sprung out of bed the following morning in one, energetic leap. She was about to meet her mother and sister for her wedding dress fitting. After brewing coffee and eating breakfast, she darted straight to the Bridal Paradise boutique in town.

"Mom, Tani, I'm sorry you had to wait for me. This is probably not the best day for my fitting." She shook her head. "I've been bloated constantly for the past few weeks. But, I'm excited to get the dress going."

"Tani and I only got here a couple of minutes ago. And, you look beautiful. Try not to worry. I know the dress will fit you like a glove."

Darcy, their bubbly and kind-hearted bridal consultant came traipsing into the waiting area.

"Hello, ladies. This is an exciting day. Your gorgeous dress is waiting for you, Ivy!...Let me take you to the dressing room."

The trio followed Darcy down a chandelier lit hallway. The scent of French perfume wafted at them.

Ivy gasped when she saw her dress. The only thing curbing her excitement was that she had been experiencing abdominal pain for days now. Fortunately, the sensation was mild and intermittent enough that she was able to push the pain out of her mind and proceed with her daily routine.

The store owner had managed to make the bridal boutique look both opulent and inviting. The walls were painted in pastel hues. Large, gold framed mirrors were on display throughout the store allowing the future brides a perfect vantage point of their dresses from every angle.

Natural light filtered through the store's floor to ceiling windows.

Ivy donned the dress of her dreams. She felt a distinct tightness through the waistline. Other than that, the dress fit her perfectly.

Her mother and Tani both teared up when they entered the changing room. A strapless, ice-white, satin gown with a demi-train swept the floor.

Her mother gasped. "Oh, my! You look exquisite, honey."

"I feel like this dress makes me look like a princess. I couldn't love it more. It fits perfectly other than the pull in the waist line."

Darcy chimed in. "That's very easy to correct. We will just let it out a little in that area. Let's do some adjustments and then you can come back for a follow-up fitting. We still have plenty of time since your wedding isn't for another five months."

"You always have a way of calming me, Darcy. Thank you. That sounds like a good plan."

They left for lunch at a nearby restaurant. Once their seafood salads were ordered, Ivy finally had a chance to look at her phone.

"That's odd, I haven't heard from Brett a single time today."

Tani shrugged. "I'm sure he's just busy with law school...Know they have grueling schedules in those types of programs...You remember Tammy? She was a friend of mine in high school. Well, she graduated from law school. Tani chuckled. "She pretty much would go radio silent every time finals or mid-terms came up... Not a big deal."

"You're right. I just need to chill. After all, I'll be his wife in a matter of months. Ivy smiled and shook her head. "Still sometimes feel like I need to pinch myself."

During the meal, Ivy suddenly felt a searing pain knife through her stomach. She was unable to suppress a scream and she reached out for her mother's hand.

"Oh no! What's going on, honey?"

"I've been having stomach pain lately but... this feels much worse. I'm in agony. She tried to take a deep breath. "Need to get to the E.R. I'm having the worst pain." Ivy fumbled her words out between raspy efforts.

4

The triage nurse immediately took Ivy back to an examining room. Her blood pressure, pulse and oxygen were monitored. A doctor entered the room just minutes later.

"Ms. Lane, I'm Dr. Andrews. We're going to hook you up to an IV and start you on some pain medication. While Terry does that, I will ask you a few questions. Let's figure out what's going on."

"Thank you, doctor."

"Could you describe your symptoms?"

"I've had on and off pain in my stomach for weeks…and I've been distinctly bloated. I was having lunch with my family just now and, all of a sudden, I felt a sharp pain in my abdomen."

"Any changes in your bowel movements lately?"

"I've been more constipated for months and I've seen blood when I go to the bathroom for some time."

"Ok, do you feel a burning sensation when you urinate?

"No, not at all."

"Have you had any unexplained weight loss, fever or night sweats?

"I definitely haven't had weight loss. I wish. I've had some low grade fevers recently but no night sweats. I'm getting married soon... been chalking up my symptoms to being stressed. I've also been working long hours...I'm very run down. My normal caffeine intake just isn't making me feel less fatigued like it used to."

"Ok, I will page Dr. Martin, the gastroenterologist on call. We'll get an action plan going. She'll be with you shortly...In the meantime, let's get a complete medical history from you."

Dr. Andrews completed the exam just as Dr. Martin entered the room. Ivy felt at ease and liked her instantly. She was calm and warm.

Ever since Ivy was in grade school her friends referred to her as the 'Aurora reader'. They were all still young and didn't realize yet that the correct word was 'aura' not 'Aurora'.

Ivy had always had a sixth sense about people and their genuine kindness or lack thereof. In fifth grade, a substitute teacher, Mrs. Hilden came in while their teacher, Mrs. Thompson, was out on maternity leave. Despite, the lady's burst of warmth and energy, Ivy felt something was off with her. At recess, she was surprised to hear her classmates gushing about Mrs. Hilden. Everybody loved her. Ivy just couldn't get past her negative feelings. Two week later, Mrs. Hilden was arrested for domestic abuse. From then on, Ivy's classmates took her word as the gospel.

"Good afternoon, Ms. Lane. It's so nice to meet you. I've had a chance to review your medical history and symptoms. Since you have rectal bleeding, we will need to have a look. I ordered a colonoscopy."

Ivy grimaced. "That's scary. Will the procedure hurt?"

"Not at all. You'll be sedated for the duration."

"What do you suspect I have? Do you think I have cancer?"

"Based on your age and medical history I would say that's unlikely. The colonoscopy will show us if there are issues such as Crohn's Disease or Ulcerative Colitis. I noticed that both of your parents had colon polyps. We need to check for that as well. Please try not to worry. I'll keep you updated every step of the way."

Ivy felt groggy. The pain medication was finally doing its magic. She was virtually pain free and felt calm. As promised, the colonoscopy was painless.

5

Ivy curled into a fetal position in the hospital bed. Fear crept along her spine.

Dr. Martin had just reported the results of the colonoscopy. A mass in her colon had been detected. It had been biopsied and the results would be available in two to three days.

Once Dr. Martin had departed her hospital room, Ivy cried hysterically for what felt like hours. She called Brett when she was finally able to calm down enough to speak.

"Hey, Ivy, what's up?"

"Something terrible has happened. I don't even know how to tell you this. I'm in the hospital because I had excruciating pain in my stomach after the dress fitting earlier today. Mom and Tani rushed me to the E.R. They ran a bunch of tests. There's a mass in my colon. It might be cancer... How's this even possible? I'm so young and I've always been very healthy."

Ivy began to sob again. Her tears cascaded down her face.

"What? Ivy, are you serious?"

"I wouldn't joke about something like this. I know you're scheduled to visit me in two weeks. Is there any chance you can come see me earlier than that?"

"Wow, that's a tall order. I have a lot of tests coming up next week."

Ivy listened in disbelief to her fiancé's cold, matter of fact tone. She finally mustered up the strength to meekly reply. "Of course, I understand how busy you are. I shouldn't have even asked."

"Listen, Ivy. My next class starts in twenty minutes. Mind if I call you later?"

"Sure, I love you, Brett."

Her fiancé didn't respond and hung up. She stared blankly out the window. Her entire

Colleen Hofstadter Hlavac

world had shifted and turned upside down in less than a single day.

The sun appeared as a fiery orb through the hospital window, gradually sinking into the sparkling sea. The last of the afternoon's golden rays danced across the hospital window. Spruce trees swayed in the distance. A pigeon landed on the window sill. Moments later, another one accompanied it. The plump bodied, small beaked birds began to strut back and forth while bobbing their heads. Then, they settled together in the corner of the ledge, clearly preparing for a night of rest. They looked content and closely bonded. Ivy sighed and pondered,

They seem so happy and carefree. When one moves a step, the other follows. I love Brett a lot but does he feel the same type of bond with me? I'm starting to feel more like a chore to him, just an item on his to-do list. Am I his everything? Yes, he proposed to me but his communication with me is waning more by the day. I need him now more than ever. I'm praying that I can regain his full attention when he visits me in a couple weeks. And, if I have cancer, will he still want to continue with our wedding?

The cheery nurse came in and offered Ivy a sedative for the night. She happily accepted and drifted off into a deep slumber soon after. Ivy had kept her ringer on high volume in case Brett called, as he had promised. Her phone never rang.

6

Brett raced over to Maya's dorm room. This was not the kind of news he could deliver via text.

She opened the door and was busting out of a tiny, turquoise colored tube top. Her cut-off jean shorts barely covered her behind. She never failed to take Brett's breath away.

Pulling him to her bed, Maya began passionately kissing him. Brett almost forgot that he had to tell her something urgently. After a vigorous kissing session, he finally recovered his composure.

"Baby, I need to tell you something."

"What? You're worrying me, Brett."

"Everything will be okay, but we have a big obstacle right now. Ivy had really bad stomach pain. They ran a bunch of tests and she has a mass in her colon. We won't know for sure if she has cancer until they run more tests."

"And, this concerns me because...?"

Brett took a breath. He had a lump forming in his throat for fear of disappointing her. Maya had a tendency to be hot-tempered when things did not go her way. She was the polar opposite of Ivy.

"I'm at a loss of what to do if she gets diagnosed with colon cancer."

"What do you mean?" Her eyes narrowed to almost a squint.

"How am I supposed to break up with a woman who is sick? Doesn't it make me kind of obligated to stay with her...at least temporarily?"

"Tell me you're kidding me? Are you seriously going to go ahead and marry that woman just because she has cancer?...What about us?"

"Of course, I would never actually go through with the wedding. That would be ludicrous. But, it'll make it much for difficult to leave her. I'll figure out something...Be patient with me. I can't lose you."

Maya sulked for the remainder of the evening.

Brett went back to his dorm feeling depressed. He felt a vein throbbing in his forehead the entire way. That vein served as his personal mood ring. For as long as he could remember, whenever he was sad, it would spring to life and visibly throb.

HOSPITAL

Ivy's abdominal pain was difficult to control even with IV pain medication. As a result, she was still in the hospital when the results of her biopsy returned two days later.

Dr. Martin entered her room and greeted her warmly.

"Well, how are we feeling today?"

Ivy detected a sadness on the physician's face despite her attempt at a genuine smile. Dr. Martin pulled up a chair next to Ivy's bedside.

"Good morning, Ivy. I hope you slept well?
"

"I slept ok. I kept waking up because of pain. My pain from a one to a ten is about a five. So, at least I'm not bent over from the discomfort like I was earlier. The medication is helpin' a lot. It's making it tolerable...Did my biopsy results come back yet?" She raised her eyebrows.

"Yes, I just received them. I came to you as soon as they were in... Unfortunately, the results do indicate colon cancer."

Ivy felt the room spinning around her.

"I believe your particular case is highly treatable. The good news is that the mass is localized to the bowel. The CAT scan indicates that it has not spread...Contrary to popular belief, the majority of patients with colon cancer can be treated and go on to live normal lives. Dr Honen, the oncologist, will see you later today. Dr Willis, a surgeon, will come by to your room later this afternoon as well. The three of us will set up a treatment plan. You're in good hands, Ivy."

Ivy was left alone with her terrifying thoughts when the doctor left. She called Brett but it went straight to his voicemail. She left a message for him with the tragic update and called her mother next.

Her mother had been at her bedside from the first moment of this nightmare. She had left to go home and get a few toiletries and shower right before Dr. Martin delivered the devastating news.

"Mom, I need you here now. Please come to the hospital."

"You're scaring me out of my mind, Ivy. What's going on?"

"Please, just get here."

Ivy disconnected the call and curled into a ball, a pillow covering her face to muffle her inconsolable sobs. Her entire body shook.

7

Brett sat at his favorite pub waiting for his best friend, Drew, to arrive. They had been friends since high school and were thrilled when they got accepted into the same law school.

"Brett, hope you haven't been waitin' long. I hit the worst traffic trying to get here."

"Not at all, Drew. Only been here for a few minutes myself."

"You sounded a little stressed in your texts to me. Is everything ok, bro?"

"Not really, I'm pretty much screwed…and I need your help."

"All ears. Spill it."

"You know how I've been seein' Maya?"

"I do and I've told you how wrong it is. Ivy is a great girl. She's so good to you and she obviously loves you. But, you're my best friend. I'll support you no matter what you decide."

"Thanks, dude...Well, here's the latest. Maya has been pressurin' me big time to call off my engagement...Been debating doing it. I love Ivy. I really do, but Maya makes my blood boil. Plus, I kind of like the idea of havin' a trophy wife. I want every guy in the room to envy me when I walk in with Maya clinging to me."

"Bro, that's so superficial!"

"I know it's wrong. You're the only one I can tell these things to. Anyway, there's more. Brace yourself...Ivy was just diagnosed with colon cancer."

"Oh, that's horrible! I knew she was getting tests done but I didn't expect her to have cancer!"

"Now I feel obligated to stick around. I'd look like such a jerk if I left her."

"Understatement!" Drew shook his head in disappointment at his friend.

I Don't

"Listen, you can't go through with a marriage just because someone is sick, but I've seen you with Ivy. I think you love her more than you realize you do." Don't trust Maya. I've always told you that. She just doesn't seem like a very nice girl to me. I think if you leave Ivy you'll live to regret it...But, what do I know? It's just a feelin' I'm gettin'...sounds like a recipe for disaster to me, bro."

"I'm heading out to visit Ivy soon. I will know better what to do then...Think I would end up really missin' her. I do know what you mean. My conversations with Maya have absolutely no depth to them. All she ever talks about are her looks and how much every guy wants her."

"Yeah, Maya is a pain...in my opinion. Go see Ivy and support her. I know you'll make the right decision."

8

Ivy was recuperating at her parent's home. Her treasured cat, Tiger, and her Leopard Gecko, Leapey, were staying with her at her childhood home as well.

Ivy received Tiger as a Christmas present when she was just eight years old. The duo had been inseparable ever since.

Leapey had been a surprise from her cousin when she had graduated from college. Whenever Ivy rested, Tiger would curl around her feet on the bed. Leapey would sit on her shoulder and snuggle against her neck for hours every evening.

Ivy was convinced that her pets worked better at easing her anxiety than a sedative.

Her parents doted on her and ensured she took her medication on time. When she wasn't resting, they would take turns holding vigil at her bedside.

"Mom, do you have the guest room ready for Brett? He's arriving tomorrow afternoon."

"I do. It's all ready. Such a shame that he can only stay for one night but at least you two will get to catch up and spend some time together."

"I guess."

"What's wrong, honey? You're usually so excited to see him."

"I need to talk, Mom."

"Of course, honey. You know that you can tell me anything."

"I feel like Brett is gradually distancing himself. He barely communicates with me. Whenever I mention our wedding...he changes the subject. The most painful part is that he seems disinterested and not concerned for my health ever since I was diagnosed with cancer."

"Ivy, I understand why you're upset but I know he loves you. I hate to make excuses for him but could this all be because he is graduating soon?"

"I suppose."

"You need to sit down with him when he's here tomorrow and have a good heart-to-heart talk with him...I bet this will all get resolved."

Ivy tossed and turned throughout the night. Her thoughts were like a hamster racing along on a wheel. She was eager to see Brett.

The darkness of night began to clear and the stars in the sky dimmed. The rising sun cast a rosy hue in Ivy's room.

As the sun began to rise higher in the sky, the colors became more vibrant with tangy oranges and cheerful violets. The golden fingers of sunlight warmed Ivy's face, calming her.

Birds began to chirp as if welcoming the morning and she finally drifted into a deep slumber.

Brett arrived right on schedule at the Bangor International Airport. He got into Ivy's car with a fake smile plastered onto his face. It appeared as if he had suffered from several nights of insomnia as well. Ivy felt a familiar pain in her chest as she noticed that he did not even bother to kiss her. She bit on her lip to suppress the onslaught of tears waiting to burst forth like a dam.

"Are you hungry, Brett? It's gettin' close to dinner time."

"Yeah, I'm starving."

Ivy took Brett to the Chart Room Restaurant. It was a favorite eatery among locals. They were seated along the pier, a coveted seating section of the establishment.

The duo gazed at their menus in silence. Ivy felt uneasy and gloomy. They ordered the Maine crab cakes as a starter course.

After, the couple enjoyed the Lobster Newburg-the tender lobster meat was served in a sauce of cream, egg yolk and sherry.

The views from their table were award winning. The rhythmic pulse of the waves helped calm Ivy's frayed nerves. The ocean was buzzing with its palpable strength. Lapping waves caressed the nearby beach and clumps of seaweed followed its lead. The water was gem-blue in color.

Bickering seagulls and comical pelicans flew overhead, occasionally dipping down to harass picnicking beachgoers.

Ivy observed a toddler squealing in delight as a hungry seagull chased her in obvious pursuit of her sandwich. She smiled to herself at the pure joy and innocence of childhood. She had been that way at one time-felt like a million years ago. Her life now was steeped in illness, anxiety and heartache. So much had changed.

Their conversation did not match the sumptuous meal. The evening felt awkward. Brett barely spoke throughout the dinner. He had not, yet, asked how she was feeling or inquired about her health status. They drove back to Ivy's parent's home in silence.

Once the strained couple was barricaded inside Ivy's childhood room, she decided it was time to dive deeper into the status of their relationship.

"Did you enjoy our evening, Brett?"
"Sure."

"That isn't very convincing. You seem so distant. Is everything ok?...Do you still want to get married?"

"I'm not distant...just have a lot on my mind with the upcoming finals."

Ivy noticed that the vein on his forehead sprung to life. She knew that was not a good sign.

Ivy struggled to remain composed.

"I have cancer. You haven't asked me once what my treatment is like, how I feel...and even what my prognosis is. It seems to me that my own fiancé should be concerned about me and our future...And, you never answered if you still want to get married."

"Of course, I do."

Brett's eyes and mouth didn't match, they were emotionless, even cold.

Ivy still deeply loved him, but she knew it was wrong to proceed with a wedding. Her health had clearly become a burden to him. She wanted a husband not a caretaker.

"Brett, I think it would be better to postpone our wedding."

He appeared unfazed by Ivy's suggestion. "Sure, if that's what you want."

"Actually, I don't want to *just* postpone our wedding. I feel like we should go our separate ways...I love you more than you will ever know. I lived and breathed to become your wife. I care about you too much to give you the extra strain of living with an ill wife."

Ivy collapsed into a heap and cried so hard that it was difficult for her to breathe. She only heard one word before Brett exited her room.

"Okay."

9

Brett took an uber to the airport and got on the first flight back home. He wore dark sunglasses on the plane. To his surprise, his eyes kept welling up.

He scolded himself.

Get a grip. Be a man. Yeah, Ivy was a great girl but it was obviously meant to end. Besides, I still have Maya. I'll go straight to her when I land. She'll be thrilled to hear that I'm no longer engaged.

Brett did not waste a minute. Once he arrived back in town, he darted to Maya's dorm.

He knocked twice.

There wasn't a response so, after a minute, Brett knocked again.

Finally, Maya peeked out of a side window.

"Brett, is that you? I thought you weren't getting back until tomorrow!"

"I took the first flight back. I have so much to tell you. You'll need to sit down to hear my big news."

"Sure, give me a minute."

Maya opened the door and invited him to her sofa.

"What's goin' on, Brett?"

"I don't even get a kiss from my favorite girl?"

"Can you just tell me your news?" She was clearly irritated.

"Ivy and I broke up!"

"What? Are you kidding?"

"No, our wedding is cancelled and we are no longer together!"

"Oh, that is great news," Maya's expression didn't change.

"We can be together now, baby."

A rough knock sounded at the front door. Maya went to open it. Before she had a chance to say a word, a man who looked liked he spent his entire life at the gym, bounded in and kissed her so hard that she almost fell over. Maya returned his passionate kisses.

Brett stared at them, his jaw dropped open. "What the hell is going on here, Maya? You're cheatin' on me with this steroid king?...Thought we were going to be together for life! I thought you loved me!"

"Huh?" The muscle man grunted and looked confused.

Brett doubted that this gentleman's I.Q. was higher than a bunny rabbit's.

Maya defiantly placed her hands on her hips. "Don't be dumb, Brett. I never loved you and you were a hell of a lot sexier when you were forbidden fruit...Now that you don't have a fiancée, you have lost all of your luster. She can have you!"

Maya laughed hysterically. Her face split into an evil sneer. At that moment, Brett no longer saw the extreme beauty he had seen in her before. She looked ugly, vile and nasty, no different than a hyena on the Savannah. Brett left Maya's dorm and walked back to his room feeling crushed and in a trance-like state.

10

The next several months were hell on Earth for Ivy. Chemotherapy treatments wreaked havoc on her health. She was chronically nauseous, fatigued and deeply depressed.

Two weeks into treatments, Ivy had been up for the entire night vomiting. She finally dozed off during the early morning hours. Mid-morning, her mother walked in with a breakfast tray.

"Good morning, honey. I know your stomach has been upset. I brought you some chicken noodle soup and saltine crackers. You can start out with them and if your tummy handles it, we can upgrade you to something more substantial."

"Thanks so much, Mom. I actually feel pretty hungry right now."

Ivy stretched and noticed something laying on her pillow.

"Oh no! Mom! My hair is all over my pillow…I'm losing my hair!"

A deluge of tears baptized Ivy's face. Crying had become her primary activity in the last few months.

"Well, it's a good thing I'm not about to be a bride. I look even worse than normal."

"Please don't talk like that, Ivy. You're a beautiful girl."

"You have to say that because you're my mother."

"Honey, I've been wanting to talk to you."

"What, Mom?"

"I understand that the last couple months have been very painful for you. I just wish you would consider going to the cancer support group at the hospital…think it would really help you. You've sealed yourself off from everyone since you broke up with Brett. You won't even let your best friend, Trevor, visit. Please, honey…At least, tell me you'll think about it? You're a fighter…always have been. Don't let Brett rob you of that trait."

"I know you're right…Been thinking about going to the support group for the last few days. It might help me to have another outlet. I need to win this fight. I can't die, Mom."

"You won't die, honey. We'll get through this together…as a family."

The following evening, Ivy spruced herself up, for the first time in months, in preparation for attending the support group. Her favorite jeans had previously been so tight that she had to lay on her bed and inhale a deep breath in order to pull them on. That was not the case this evening. The jeans seemed to swallow up her frail body. They were two sizes too large now.

This is typical. I'm finally thin and it's because I have the big C! Why should I even bother putting makeup on? It's like putting lipstick on a pig!

With Ivy's uncharacteristically bitter and negative thoughts, she stormed out of her home and drove to the hospital.

11

The gathering at the support group was larger than Ivy had expected. The facilitator welcomed her warmly as soon as she entered the conference room.

"Hello, My name is Jean and I'm the facilitator for our Wednesday night group. It's a pleasure to meet you."

"Thank you, Jean. My name is Ivy. I have colon cancer and I've never been to a support group before. I'm not sure what to expect...I'm a little nervous."

"Don't you worry about a thing, Ivy. We are all here to help each other. I bet you will form some great friendships. You can either just observe or partake in the discussion. Do whatever makes you most comfortable."

Ivy felt comforted by the soothing, soft-spoken lady. She took a seat next to her.

The hour long session passed by in a blur. Ivy heard about the battles of her fellow group members. She felt instantly bonded to them and even mustered up the courage to share her story.

"Hi, my name is Ivy. This is my first time at a support group. I was diagnosed with colon cancer pretty recently. It was a double whammy because my engagement broke up soon after my diagnosis."

There was an audible gasp of empathy when Ivy spoke. Ivy continued to share her story. The group enjoyed refreshments after the meeting concluded. A young lady approached Ivy.

"Hi Ivy, I'm Carrie. I'm happy you decided to come to our meeting. I think you'll really like coming here. At first, I was hesitant but now I can't wait for Wednesday evenings to come around."

Ivy estimated that Carrie was in her twenties as well. The two women bonded immediately.

"I had breast cancer. I finished my treatments a year ago and I'm still disease free. Thank goodness that they caught it early."

"That's wonderful to hear.

At the conclusion of the gathering Ivy turned to Carrie. "Would you like to meet for coffee tomorrow morning, Carrie?"

"Yes, I would love that. Let's meet at the Caffeine Bar next-door to the hospital at 10:00 a.m., if that works for you."

"I'll be there. See you then."

Ivy drove home and called for her mother the moment she entered the house.

"Mom, the group went so well. I don't feel nearly as alone in my cancer battle anymore. The people there are great. I'm even meeting a new friend tomorrow morning for coffee."

"Oh, honey, I can't tell you how happy that makes me."

"Mom, could we talk more in the morning? It's way past my bedtime."

Both ladies giggled and Ivy fell into the deepest and most restful slumber she had experienced in months.

The following morning she met Carrie at the coffee shop. Generally, Ivy's coffee meet ups lasted an hour or two. This meeting continued for well over four hours.

The new friends had so much in common. They spoke endlessly about their lives. Something Carrie said made Ivy lean into the table and cling on to every word.

"I'm super excited, Ivy. I just got accepted into medical school, the University of Oregon. It has always been my dream to become a dermatologist…looks like that will happen now."

"Oh, Carrie, I'm beyond impressed. Would you believe that being a doctor has always been my dream too? I put it out of my mind when my fiancé discouraged it and now I'm sick. I guess it just isn't in the cards for me."

"Are you kidding? Of course, it's in the cards. You're so young and you told me yourself that your prognosis is excellent, Ivy. You have your whole life in front of you…I say you go for it, girl. I can guide you on what steps you need to take. Assuming you have the prerequisites from your undergraduate program, your next step would be to take an MCAT prep class. The MCAT is kind of like the SAT but much more intense and geared for entering medical school."

Ivy left her coffee meet up with a renewed pep in her step. She had always been driven and hard working but she had let Brett, and now cancer, stifle that within her. She was back and more driven than ever. Ivy was determined to start living every day to the fullest. In the car ride home, she had time to ponder everything she had learned from her new friend.

No more, pity parties. Yeah, I have been dealt some really lousy cards lately but it's time for me to move forward. Of course, there will still be days when I feel physically ill. I need to expect that and be more patient and loving to myself, treat myself as well as I treated Brett.

12

Months later, Ivy had completed her chemotherapy treatments. She had an appointment this afternoon with Dr. Honen, her oncologist. It was the moment of truth.

She was about to find out if she was cancer free. With sweaty palms and a racing heartbeat, Ivy was called to the physician's examining room. Dr. Honen did not leave her waiting for long.

"Good afternoon, Ivy! How are you feeling?"

"Hi, Dr Honen, I've actually been feeling much better. I still get nauseous and fatigued but it's happening way less often. Super nervous right now to hear the results of my recent CAT scan and blood work."

"Don't be nervous. I have a lot of good news for you. Your CAT scan is clear and your blood tests are all within the normal range. At this point, you are cancer-free."

"Seriously?"

"Very serious! Your tumor has responded remarkably well to the treatments. We will, of course, need to continue to closely monitor you but you are heading in the right direction."

Ivy teared up from feeling pure elation.

"I can't think of better news, doctor. I've actually been preparing for the MCAT and also, at the same time, applying to almost two dozen medical schools. If I'm lucky enough to get accepted, do you feel that, health wise, it would be okay for me to leave this area to attend med school?"

"I don't see that being an issue. There are oncologists on staff at all major hospitals. They can continue to monitor you for the fours years you are in medical school...I'm really proud of you, Ivy. You had mentioned to me in the past how much you wanted to be a physician. I'm betting you'll be a great one."

"Thank you, doctor...You inspired me! You're always so calming and knowledgeable. I've wanted to be a doctor for as long as I can remember, but seeing how much of a difference a doctor's kindness and care can help in the healing process, confirmed that's the career for me all the more."

Ivy practically skipped out of the doctor's office. She could not wait to share the good news with her family and friends.

13

Three months later, Ivy was checking emails before she had to go to the hospital for her Wednesday support group. As she scanned her inbox, she spotted an email from Temple Medical School. Shivers climbed up and down her spine. This was the moment of truth. Temple was one of her top choices. Would she get accepted or rejected?

Dear Ms. Lane,

Congratulations! On behalf of the admissions committee, it is my honor and privilege to share with you that you have been admitted into the Lewis Katz School of Medicine at Temple University.

Ivy had to rub her eyes to ensure that they were not playing tricks on her. Her parents were not at home but she felt so besides herself with ecstasy that she blurted the outstanding news to Tiger and Leapey. Tiger cowered and crawled under the desk when Ivy let out a shriek.

I've been accepted into medical school! I'm going to Philadelphia! My friends at the group will be excited to hear my news!

Ivy dashed to the meeting and volunteered to be the first member to share for the session. The entire support group cheered and gave Ivy a standing ovation when she announced her acceptance into medical school.

Jean chimed in, "I've never had any doubt that you could do it. I still remember how nervous you were on your first night here...all those months ago. You had been newly diagnosed and had just suffered a broken engagement. Look how far you've come!"

The group erupted into hoots and hollers.

Once the room quieted, Jean continued. "Ivy's acceptance into medical school is a reminder that, as scary as a cancer diagnosis is, with lots of love and support, we can actually continue to pursue our dreams. You've got this, Ivy! You're going to make an incredible and caring physician."

14

The following months passed by in a flash as Ivy prepared for her move to Philadelphia. She had been texting and face-timing her future roommate, Sabrina. She was from Arizona and had wanted to be a doctor for years as well. The duo seemed to click well.

The day had finally arrived. Ivy and her parents flew to Philadelphia. They rented a car and headed for the university. The headlights of their sedan cut through the pinkish dusk.

The city of brotherly love was coming alive with music and a kaleidoscope of shimmering lights which reflected off of the windows of the buildings. The evening sun cast long shadows on the ground. The drive was as quiet as an empty church-Ivy was lost in thought.

So, this is it. I'm about to start a new chapter in my life. Philly will be my home for the next four years. I worked hard to get to this point. I'm nervous. What if I can't keep up with the course load? What if I fail?

Ivy's mother had always been intuitive. Almost as if on cue, she interrupted her daughter's thoughts.

"How are you feeling, Ivy? You're about to embark on a big adventure."

"I'm anxious. For years, I wanted to be a doctor but I put those dreams to the side after Brett proposed. From that point on, all my energy went into saving money for our life together and preparing for the wedding. That obviously all blew up when our relationship ended. I'm proud of myself for getting back on track. Sure, I was horribly heartbroken but I somehow managed to dust myself off and put my efforts back towards recovering from my illness and preparing to go to medical school. I still think about Brett sometimes. I miss him but I would rather realize now that he wasn't the one for me rather than ten or twenty years down the road."

"I couldn't agree with you more, honey. I realize the broken engagement hurt you terribly. I know how much you loved him. Sadly, he just wasn't attentive to you after you were diagnosed. Brett wasn't there when you needed him the most. You deserve someone who will treat you like a queen."

"Thanks, Mom. For now, dating is secondary. I need to focus on my studies. If someone great comes along, then fine, but it isn't my top priority."

They pulled into the dormitory parking lot and located Ivy's room number. Her father swung the heavy, wooden door open.

The room was unoccupied but it was clear that Sabrina had already arrived. Her luggage was placed on top of one of the beds. The room was mid-sized and minimally decorated. Two beds, desks, halogen lights and a small, metal garbage can filled the space.

Ivy could feel her heart pounding. She anxiously peered out of the window. A bustling cheesesteak shop was across the street. Its obnoxious, neon, scarlet-red sign 'Phil's Cheesesteaks' flashed into Ivy's room.

Just then, Sabrina burst into their dorm room. Her energy and enthusiasm was infectious. Horn-rimmed glasses framed her lively, close-set, pale blue eyes. Her silky hair tumbled to her shoulders in autumnal hues.

Sabrina's pasty skin hinted at her inactive lifestyle. Ivy was aware that Sabrina spent the majority of her days cooped inside studying. She had admitted to Ivy that she had never seen the inside of a gym and rarely even taken a casual walk. The majority of her young life had been dedicated to preparing for medical school. The roommates embraced and hit it off instantly.

"Ivy, I'm so excited to finally meet you. Feels like we are old friends since we've been face-timing so much."

"I agree, Sabrina. Can't believe we're finally face to face in real life...These are my parents, Warner and Alice. We just got here a few minutes ago."

"It's so nice to meet you all. My parents brought me here a few hours ago.

Warner chimed in. "Well, it's so nice to finally meet you…You ladies must be hungry?"

"Maybe a little," admitted Sabrina.

"Why don't I run across the street to Phil's Cheesesteaks and get us some sustenance."

"That sounds like a great idea, Dad. I've heard so much about Philadelphia's excellent cheesesteaks…love to try one."

"Say no more. I'll go get us some now. Alice, care to join me?"

"Love to."

The night was filled with delicious food and great conversation. Ivy's new chapter was off to an excellent start.

15

TWO MONTHS LATER

Ivy was exiting her Microscopic Anatomy class when one of her classmates approached her.

"Hey, Ivy! Do you feel ready for the test we are having in class next week?"

"Not yet, Justin. I'm hoping if I cram for the next several days, I'll get there though."

"Would you like to study with me? My brother graduated from Temple Med last spring. He kept all of the notes from his classes. They've been helpful to me so far."

"Thanks so much! Would love that."

"We could meet in one of the smaller conference rooms in the Simmy and Harry Ginsburg Library. Would 7:00 p.m. work for you?"

"Yeah, perfect. I'll see you then...and thanks again."

Ivy darted to her dorm and burst into the room. Her face was flushed with excitement.

"Guess what, Sabrina?"

"What? Are you okay? Your face looks so red."

"I'm more than okay. Do you remember when I told you about the cute guy from my anatomy class? Justin?"

"Of course. The one with sun streaked hair and about as tall as a pro-basketball player?"

"That's the one." Ivy giggled.

"Well, he just came up to me after class and asked me to do a study date tonight!"

"Really? I'm so excited for you. There are so many people in that class. You obviously caught his attention since he asked you to meet up."

"Do you really think so? I get it's just a study date but it's a start. This is the first man I've been even slightly interested in since Brett and I broke up."

"It's a great start and you obviously have a lot in common since you both are studying to be doctors."

"That's true, don't want to get ahead of myself. We'll see what happens."

At 7:00 p.m. sharp, Ivy arrived at the library. Frustration crept in and she nervously checked her watch at 7:20. Finally, just after 7:30, Justin meandered into the library. Perhaps she had heard the time incorrectly?

Ivy saw him enter the library and he approached her. "Sorry, Ivy, I'm a little late because I was on the phone with my best friend from high school...totally lost track of time."

Masking her disappointment, Ivy mumbled, "Of course, no problem. Well, shall we dive into it, Justin?"

"Sounds good to me. I forgot to bring my brother's notes, but we can wing it."

Ivy was pleased that despite the delay, they worked well together and covered a lot of ground. To her relief, she felt more prepared for the upcoming quiz because of their study session.

"Ivy, my friend, Tom, is having a get-together at his place next weekend. Would love it if you'd join us."

"Sounds like fun...I'd like that."

Great, Tom's place is on Cecil B. Moore Avenue. Not sure if you're familiar with that area?"

"I know exactly where it is. I'll be there."

"Cool. I had better get going. I still need to hit the gym tonight. Thanks for the study session. It was nice."

"I enjoyed it and I feel like I'm finally getting a grasp of the material. We should do our study sessions more often, Justin."

"I agree. Have a good night...and bundle up. It's cold out there."

Ivy exited the library and began the trek back to her dorm room. The frosty, jet-black night seemed to beckon her to get home and go to sleep. Her coat was no match for the icy wind, which found every opportunity to creep in to un-tightened seams.

Ivy's breath formed ghost like figures in the unforgiving air, her earlobes burned in the breeze. A dull ache in Ivy's abdomen sprung to life. Ever since her cancer diagnosis, these aches and pains had the power to fill Ivy with dread and panic.

I'm sure it's nothing. Who doesn't have aches and pains sometimes? Besides, I'm due for another check up next week. The doctor will make sure that everything is still in order.

16

Ivy went to her new oncologist, Dr. Hansen, at Temple University Hospital. He ordered a battery of tests to ensure that Ivy was still disease-free. She reported the stomach pain she had been experiencing recently.

A week later, alarm engulfed Ivy when she received a call from the doctor's office.

"Good morning, Ivy. Your test results are back and Dr. Hansen was wondering if you could come in this afternoon for a follow-up meeting."

"Yes, I can make that. Thank you. See you then."

As soon as she disconnected the call, she phoned her mother.

"Mom, I'm scared."

"Why, sweetheart? What's going on?"

"You know how I had a bunch of tests done to check why I'm having abdominal pain?"

"Yes, have you gotten the results back yet?"

"That's just it. The nurse called and said that the doctor wants to see me this afternoon. What if my cancer is back?"

"I'm sure that's not what it is. They probably just want to go over the results with you."

"But, why so quickly? I have never had the doctor office call me and try to get me to come in the same day!"

"Honey, you're reading into things. For all you know, the doctor had a cancellation and they could squeeze you in earlier than normal."

"You're right. I'll call you and tell you what he said the moment my appointment is over."

"Please do. I'll be praying."

Ivy was seated in the doctor's office waiting room, perusing the latest issue of Vogue Magazine. Her palms were so sweaty that the glossy pages kept sticking to her skin.

"Ms. Lane, Dr. Hansen is able to see you now."

Ivy was escorted back to an examining room.

The walls were covered with an array of autumn landscapes of the Pennsylvania countryside.

Dr. Hansen entered the room moments later. From his general demeanor, Ivy was hopeful that he had good news for her.

"It's nice to see you, Ivy. I have great news. All of your tests indicate that you are cancer-free. I suspect the abdominal pain you are having could be from not getting enough fiber and exercise. I'd stock up on lentils, whole grains, fruits and drink plenty of water. I realize you're a busy medical student but if you could even get in some walking a few days a week, it would help. Just a twenty minute walk could make a difference with your symptoms. Plus, walking helps relieve stress."

"Thank you, Dr. Hansen. I can't tell you how relieved I am. I'll make a point of taking better care of myself. I tend to get wrapped up in my studies. Then, unfortunately, I skip meals and forget about exercise...Not a good combo."

"I get it. I remember how intense medical school was. Just a few tweaks should make you feel much better."

17

SPRINGTIME

Ivy had been casually dating Justin for almost six months. She was feeling particularly frustrated one afternoon and confided in her roommate, whom she now counted as one of her best friends.

"Can we take a quick study break and talk, Sabrina?"

"Of course, what's going on?

"Justin can just be so flaky. It has been really grating on my nerves lately. He has cancelled out on our last three dates. We're supposed to spend the day hiking tomorrow in the Pocono Mountains. We'll see if he doesn't back out again."

"He does seem pretty flaky. Have you two had the talk yet? Are you exclusive?"

"Justin has made it crystal clear to me that he's interested in dating other women also. I assumed he would change his mind and want to commit by the six month mark, but that hasn't happened...At least, he's being honest. Right?"

"I guess, Ivy, but you deserve to be treated like a queen. Don't settle. I'm going to go over there and clobber Justin if I hear one more time that he showed up late or cancelled one of your dates."

"You're a great friend, Sabrina. Not sure what I would do without you."

"Well, you'll never have to find out."

The friends went back to poring over their books. Lights were out by 10:00 p.m. Ivy fell asleep the moment her head hit the pillow. The fatigue of endless study sessions caught up with her.

As promised, Justin arrived the next morning to pick up Ivy for their day excursion. She was pleasantly surprised.

Maybe there is hope for us after all!

The drive from Philadelphia to the Pocono Mountains took just under two hours. The couple passed quaint historic towns and a variety of landscapes ranging from rivers to old growth forests to bubbling wetlands.

Justin broke the silence, "Today, we're going to the Appalachian Trail. Did you know that it's the longest hiking-only footpath in the world?…Over two thousand miles long!"

"Really? That's so cool. I don't think my hiking boots are quite good enough to walk that far."

Laughter filled the car.

"We'll only walk about six miles today, Ivy…think you'll love it. I've been here a bunch of times. I tend to see different sights every time I go. There's a bunch of wildlife…seen coyotes, deer, bears and even the Eastern Copperhead Rattlesnake!"

"I love animal sightings. The snake part sounds kind of creepy though. How close did you come to it?"

"I've seen a few of them. The snakes were probably about ten feet away from me. They won't bother you if you don't bother them."

"Ok, that makes me feel a little better."

They arrived at the trailhead soon after.

"You weren't kiddin', Justin. This place is gorgeous."

"Right? You haven't seen anything yet. We'll stop at a waterfall in a bit for lunch."

They trudged through a heavily forested wilderness. The ground was covered with a blanket of brown leaves and melting snow. As they exited the tree line, a gust of icy wind blew across the trail. The terrain became steep. Fir and spruce trees once again enveloped the hikers.

Ivy tried to distract her fatigued body with thoughts of the picnic they would soon enjoy.

"Ivy, let's hike through this field of dandelions. It's a shortcut to our lunch spot."

"No complaints here. I'm starting to feel winded."

As they cleared the dandelion field, and rejoined the trail, they stopped in their tracks.

"Damn, is that a bear?" Justin shouted.

The animal whipped its head around at the sound of their approach. Its eyes glinted as it snorted in their direction. They were only a few yards away from the massive beast which Ivy estimated to be about five hundred pounds. They were in momentary shock.

The bear stared at them silently. If only that would have lasted. It slapped the ground with his paws. Each nail was four inches long and thick as cigars. The bear snorted again and snapped its teeth together like a trap just sprung by a tasty morsel.

Remembering what he had read about bear attacks, Justin stretched upward and made himself appear as large as possible. The bear did not seem impressed as he charged at them at lightning speed. In the last moment, the animal veered off to the side. It never let Ivy and Justin out of its sights.

"Justin, what are we going to do?He's going to charge again!"

"I'll continue to make myself look extra tall. Very slowly, take out your cell phone and call 911."

"Ok."

In slow motion, Ivy reached for her phone. Her hand was shaking uncontrollably. Justin never relaxed his extended stance.

"Oh no, no service here."

"Was afraid of that. Reach and take the phone from my back pocket. By a miracle, my phone will have some reception."

Ivy reached for Justin's phone. To her horror, he did not have any reception either. Just then, the bear charged again, grunting as he approached the horrified hikers. Once again, the animal veered off before attacking.

For at least another hour, the bear repeatedly bluffed and charged before pulling off to the side.

Ivy felt dehydrated and weak from hunger. She thought to herself sorrowfully,

Tell me I didn't survive cancer only to end up getting mauled to death by a bear. This can't be happening to us. What are the odds? There is barely even one bear attack in the United States

a year. We have a higher chance of getting struck by lightning.

Just then, Ivy's grim thoughts were interrupted by a pack of hikers exiting the dandelion field. They were a loud and lively group of young adults. The bear's eyes grew large. He startled and bounded in the opposite direction. They were finally safe.

"That was way too close for my liking, Ivy. Why don't we get back to the car, have lunch there and then just drive back to Temple and call it a day."

"I couldn't agree more. This date gave me enough adventure to last a lifetime."

Ivy released a big sigh of relief when she finally got back to her dorm room.

18

It was a humid, spring evening. Ivy was alone in the dorm room, staring out at Phil's Cheesesteak shop. As usual, the line for his well known subs snaked around the corner. It was already 8:00 p.m.

Justin had promised he would pick her up at 6:30 p.m. so they could go and grab a bite to eat at a local Italian eatery. She started texting to ask his whereabouts an hour ago. He had not responded to her yet.

Just then, Sabrina entered the dorm.

"Tell me you aren't still here! Did Justin flake again?"

"Of course, he did. This is getting old. Heck, it became old months ago...think I've hit my limit."

"What do you mean, Ivy?"

"I swore when Brett broke my heart that I would never let anyone treat me disrespectfully again. I deserve better. Mom always says that they will treat you they way you allow them to... I'm done. I won't ever again waste my time on a man who doesn't respect me."

"I'm proud of you and I agree. He isn't worth the salt in your tears."

The following morning, Ivy texted Justin and told him that she needed to talk to him immediately. They agreed to meet at one of the campus coffee shops. Not surprisingly, her soon to be ex-boyfriend showed up twenty minutes late.

"Hey, Ivy, what's the emergency?" Justin posed the question in an irritated tone as he sat down in the booth across from her.

"No emergency, I just wanted to talk. We've been seeing each other for a while. You're a great guy but I just don't think you are the man for me."

"Oh, what brought this on?"

Ivy could tell that his ego was bruised much more than his heart was.

"I went though hell when my engagement with Brett ended. I never want to be in a situation like that again. I've learned to look for clues if I'm not compatible with someone. Somebody I can depend on is important to me...More often than not, you cancel our plans or show up late."

"That's fine, Ivy, if that's what you want."

"I think it's for the best."

Ivy exited the coffee shop. She felt proud of herself and realized how much her self-confidence had improved since the days she acted like a doormat with Brett.

I will never again let any man undermine my worth. I would much rather be alone than in an unhealthy relationship. One day, I want a marriage like my parents have. They support and love each other unconditionally.

19

THIRTY YEARS LATER

It was the first Saturday Ivy had taken off in months. She was a self-described workaholic. Reaching for today's issue of the New York Times on her driveway, she went back into her impressive home and sat on the glossy leather sofa.

As anticipated, Ivy stared down at her own ecstatic looking face from the front page of the paper. The headline read, "Groundbreaking Heart Surgeon." She beamed with pride as she continued to read the article.

78

Doctor Ivy Lane, world renowned cardiac surgeon, is a pioneer for the percutaneous aortic valve replacements. This procedure allows the replacing of the heart's aortic valve through the blood vessels, as opposed to open heart surgery.

As she was perusing the long awaited article, Ivy's husband, Jack, burst into the kitchen.

"Sweetheart, is that the Times? Did the article about you finally get printed?" Jack's eyes were brimming with love and pride.

"It sure is, honey. I can't believe they finally published the article."

"Nobody deserves success more than you do. You've worked so hard for this. I knew when we met in the Cardiac Surgery Fellowship that you were going places."

"You always have believed in me, Jack. I thank my lucky stars every day that I met you. I didn't know what real love was until we started dating.

Ivy had met Jack in the first month of her fellowship. They became fast friends and fell in love shortly thereafter. He was always there for her, supporting her and loving her. Jack proposed eight months later.

As Ivy walked down the church aisle to him on their wedding day, tears filled her eyes. Tani was Ivy's maid of honor. Trevor, Sabrina and Carrie were also in the wedding party.

She knew then that any heartache she had encountered in her past was well worth it to get to this moment. It was all a learning experience. She did not hold any ill will again Brett or Justin. They were valuable teaching moments for her.

Jack and Ivy had a beautiful marriage. They chose not to have children since they wanted to give a hundred percent to their careers and to each other. To the couple's great relief, Ivy remained cancer-free. She excelled in cardiac surgery and became world renowned for her discoveries. Ivy's mother continued to be her closest confidant and friend.

20

Ivy rushed to the hospital cafeteria during her lunch break. She settled into a corner booth and started her Caesar salad. Half way through her meal, an older gentleman hesitantly approached her table.

"Ivy?"

"Yes?"

"You don't recognize me?"

"I'm sorry...Who are you?

"Brett,...Brett Westin."

Ivy tried to mask her surprise. She would have never known it was her former fiancé if he had not introduced himself.

"Oh wow, hello Brett. It's nice to bump into you again after all these years."

"I know. It's so exciting to see you, Ivy. You're more ravishing than ever. What's your secret?"

"Thank you. My secret is probably a combination of being happy in life and also being very active at work still."

"Whatever you're doing, it's definitely working. May I join you for a few minutes?"

"Of course, Brett. Have a seat."

"I'm at the hospital because I've been bringing my sister to her oncology appointments. She has metastatic breast cancer. During her treatments, I have downtime, so, I often come in here. I never thought I would have the opportunity to be face to face with you again."

Ivy noticed Brett's eyes continually filling up with tears. He seemed embarrassed by his display of emotion and claimed he was suffering from seasonal allergies. Ivy knew this was not the case.

"Listen, Ivy, I need to tell you something. I've been wanting to say this to you for decades."

"Oh?" Ivy braced herself for what was about to get divulged to her.

"Not giving a hundred percent to our relationship all those years ago was the biggest mistake of my life. I was a young fool. You deserved to be treated like pure gold. I wasn't there for you when you needed me the most, when you were very ill...Can you ever forgive me?"

Ivy was always kind to the core and this moment was no different. Yes, he hurt her to the highest level, left her alone and scared when she was battling cancer, but she persevered and became strong and brave despite the obstacles.

"Of course, I forgive you, Brett. I know that we were very young. Please forgive yourself too. Life is too short to carry around extra burdens."

"I truly loved you, Ivy. I still do. I never stopped. I was a selfish jerk."

"I appreciate your kind words, Brett. Thank you. Our time together was very special to me and I was definitely in love with you. Now, if you"ll excuse me. My lunch break is over. I need to get back to the operating room."

Brett's face dropped. Tears flowed down his tired, sun damaged skin. He attempted to regain his composure.

"Of course, I know you're a busy physician. Have a wonderful afternoon. I sure hope that I'll bump into you again soon."

Ivy thanked him and started to exit the cafeteria. She heard Brett stammer,

"Ivy? Do you ever have any regrets that we didn't get married…any at all?

She turned to look at him.

"I don't…" She shrugged and walked away.

THE END

I Don't

Preview

Colleen's next exciting murder mystery novel
Terror Forest

1

DEAL, NEVADA

Chants rose into the hot, summer night air like helium balloons escaping their confines. The cult members raised their arms and chanted in unison.

A makeshift altar had been set up in a grove of redwood trees. The members appeared to be in a trance-like state.

Standing in a crescent moon configuration, they

were all dressed in black. An exceptionally tall figure, cloaked in a black robe, led the ceremony. Candles perched on top of the altar illuminated his outline.

After the ceremony concluded the leader, Abbott, announced updates to the members of the cult.

"I'm not liking our numbers at all. We haven't added new members in some time. I understand that living in the small town of Deal limits how many newcomers we can find. But, we've got to step up our efforts. We need to thrive and ultimately become the rulers of the world. Let's mainly focus on recruitment right now...Another thing, sacrificing Belle London was foolish. She was way too high profile of a person. Think about it, folks! You kill the homecoming queen of Deal High School and we all suffer the consequences. You started a frenzy with law enforcement! They're asking a lot of questions...Now, there's even going to be a crime show documentary about Belle's death. This is the type of attention our cult just doesn't need!"

Abbott adjourned the meeting and the cult members silently drifted off into the undergrowth of the dense, Nevada forest.

LINDEN, NEW JERSEY

Winter Wells sprung up from her desk as the final bell at Linden High School rang. She exited the building feeling a combination of excitement and nostalgia.

Her long, wavy, caramel colored hair bounced along her back. Winter's crystal-blue eyes blinked away the harsh, afternoon sunlight.

She had just completed her junior year. It was finally summer vacation.

The beautiful, fun-loving teen had lived in Linden, New Jersey her entire life.

Recently, her minister father had received a job offer he could not refuse. Mr. Wells was hired to be the lead minister in a church in Deal, Nevada. Unlike his current job, he would now also hold a supervisory role.

Winter turned to her best friend, Jules. "I'm so proud of my dad but I still can't believe we are moving as far away as Nevada. That is clear across the country!...I've been friends with you since preschool. I'm going to miss you so much, Jules."

"Can't believe it either, Winter. I'm going to go through withdrawal symptoms without you... been begging my parents to look for jobs in Nevada so we can move there too. Mom and Dad look at me like I'm crazy whenever I suggest it. They've both been working at the same jobs for the past twenty years. But, you just never know. Stranger things have happened. I won't give up. I'll keep pushing them."

"I'll keep my fingers crossed, Jules. I just can't imagine starting a new school and you not being there."

"I know, Winter. If all else fails I guess there's always FaceTime. We can talk every single day. It will be almost like we are in the same town...And, I can come visit during Thanksgiving break. Dad promised me that I could."

"I'd love that so much. Who knows? Moving to Deal could end up being the start of many interesting adventures."

Colleen Hofstadter Hlavac

OTHER NOVELS FROM COLLEEN HLAVAC

THE STALKER IN THE DESERT

LIQUID DECEPTIONS

ACKNOWLEDGEMENTS

To Andrea and Christian Hofstadter, for being the models and providing the cover photo.

SEE MORE AT:

www.colleenhlavac.com